STARRY SKIES AND
FIREFLIES

the FRIENDSHIP garden

STARRY SKIES AND FIREFLIES

by Jenny Meyerhoff
illustrated by Éva Chatelain

ALADDIN
New York London Toronto Sydney New Delhi

ALADDIN
An imprint of Simon & Schuster Children's Publishing Division
1230 Avenue of the Americas, New York, New York 10020
First Aladdin paperback edition February 2017
Text copyright © 2017 by Simon & Schuster, Inc.
Illustrations copyright © 2017 by Éva Chatelain
Also available in an Aladdin hardcover edition.
All rights reserved, including the right of reproduction in whole or in part in any form.
ALADDIN and related logo are registered trademarks of Simon & Schuster, Inc.
For information about special discounts for bulk purchases, please contact
Simon & Schuster Special Sales at 1-866-506-1949 or business@simonandschuster.com.
The Simon & Schuster Speakers Bureau can bring authors to your live event. For more information or to book an event contact the Simon & Schuster Speakers Bureau at
1-866-248-3049 or visit our website at www.simonspeakers.com.
Book designed by Laura Lyn DiSiena
The text of this book was set in Century Expanded LT Std.
Manufactured in the United States of America 0117 OFF
10 9 8 7 6 5 4 3 2 1
Library of Congress Control Number 2016951741
ISBN 978-1-4814-7052-0 (hc)
ISBN 978-1-4814-7051-3 (pbk)
ISBN 978-1-4814-7053-7 (eBook)

STARRY SKIES AND FIREFLIES

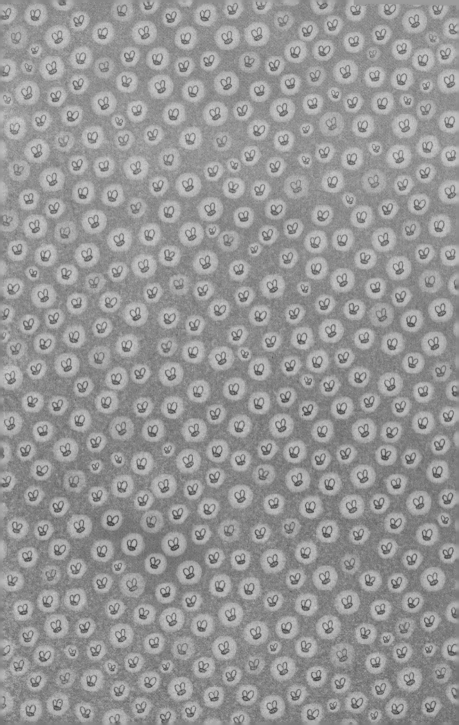

CONTENTS

CHAPTER 1

THE PICKY PICKERS PICNIC

Anna swung a wicker basket by her side as she skipped down the block ahead of her father and her brother, Collin. It had been four whole days since she'd been to the Friendship Garden. Up ahead, Anna could see the gate for Shoots and Leaves, the community garden that hosted her school's garden club. Anna's skip turned into a gallop. She couldn't wait to get there.

Since a garden needed tending all summer long, different families took turns weeding and watering the plants in the Friendship Garden. Then, every Monday evening, all the families would meet at the garden to pick whatever was ripe and eat a picnic dinner together. Anna called it the Picky Pickers Picnic. She liked making up names for things.

When Anna stepped inside the gates of Shoots and Leaves, her eyes darted around until she saw a girl with glasses and wavy black hair over by the chicken coop.

"Kaya!" Anna shouted, and both girls ran toward each other and spun around in a huge hug. Anna let her basket fall to the ground.

"Dios mio!" Kaya's grandmother, Daisy, said with a laugh. "You act like long lost *amigas*,

but you just saw each other a few days ago."

"During school and camp we're used to seeing each other every day," Kaya explained. "Three days is a long time."

"Especially for best friends," Anna added, hugging Kaya again.

"Look what I found!" Kaya said. "I couldn't wait to show you." She held up a shiny purple star-shaped charm, the kind found on a bracelet. "It was sitting on the post of the chicken coop."

"It's so pretty." Anna watched as the star caught a beam of sunlight and sparkled at her.

"Well, I hope you can stop hugging and chatting long enough to help us pick the cabbage and carrots." Daisy turned them both to face the garden. "No dinner until the work is done!"

Kaya put her charm in her pocket, Anna picked up her basket, and both girls walked to the raised garden bed where a few people were already picking vegetables. Mr. Hoffman, Anna's teacher from the previous school year, was picking cabbage with Maria, the president of Shoots and Leaves. Beside them, Maria's daughter, Simone, and Simone's best friend, Imani, helped.

Anna and Kaya sat down near Simone and Imani to help pick the cabbage.

"First, you have to feel around the head of cabbage," Simone told them. "Like this." She pressed her fingers around the dense ball of leaves.

"I've picked cabbage before," Anna started to say. "So you don't need to—"

"When you find the stem, cut it." Simone

had a tool that looked like the safety knife Anna used when carving pumpkins on Halloween. She sawed back and forth at the base of the cabbage until the head popped off.

"Then you can peel the outer leaves away, like this." Simone spoke very slowly. "Be careful not to cut yourselves." She handed two safety knives to Anna and Kaya, then walked to her mother's garden plot.

Anna kneeled at the edge of the bed, then reached down to the base of a cabbage.

"We're not babies," she pointed out to Kaya.

"Yeah," Kaya agreed, starting to saw through a cabbage of her own. "Just because she's going to start middle school in a couple of weeks, she acts like she's a million years older than us now."

Anna giggled. "Maybe we should start calling her Granny Simone."

Kaya started to laugh too, but just then Mr. Hoffman tapped his trowel against the edge of a flowerpot to get everyone's attention. Anna set her safety knife on the edge of the garden bed and listened.

"Thank you all for your dedication this summer. Without you, the Friendship Garden would be an overgrown mess. To show my appreciation, I'm going to host an end-of-summer party in the garden for everyone."

"Yes!" Anna and Kaya exclaimed. Anna and Kaya hugged each other. A party in the garden sounded like the perfect end to Anna's summer.

"What kind of party will it be?" Collin asked. "I like costume parties. I already have a bee costume."

"I was thinking you kids could decide what kind of party you wanted," Mr. Hoffman said. "After all, it's your reward for being such great help. A costume party sounds fun. Does anyone else have a suggestion?"

Anna jumped up. "I do! We could have a Sprinkler Splash! We could all wear our bathing suits, turn on the garden sprinklers, and do our party games in the spray. It could be like a water park, but with water balloons and water sports. That way it would be a party for the kids and a party for our flowers *and* vegetables. They'd love to drink up all that water."

Out of the corner of her eye, Anna saw Simone elbow Imani in the ribs, then roll her eyes. "Some of us might be too old for running through sprinklers," Simone called out to the group.

Anna felt her cheeks grow warm. She hadn't been suggesting they run through sprinklers, just that they have the sprinklers on during the party. It wasn't the same thing.

"I think we should do something that would be fun for *everyone*," Simone continued. "Like have a campout in the garden overnight. Everyone could bring a tent, and we could make a campfire in our fire pit and roast marshmallows and tell ghost stories."

Anna swallowed the lump that lodged in

her throat when she heard the word *ghost*. She couldn't see what scary stories had to do with gardening.

"Maybe we could have a Royal Garden Party, with cucumber sandwiches and iced tea with mint from the garden," Anna suggested. She could just picture how bright and cheery it would be, not dark and creepy like a campout. "We could all dress up like kings and queens," she added.

Anna stopped talking for a moment and waited to hear what everyone thought of her idea, but no one said anything. She looked at Kaya, but Kaya only shrugged one shoulder and wrinkled up half of her nose. "I guess that would be fun," she said. "But I've always wanted to try camping. I've never slept outside before!"

"I want to do a campout!" Collin shouted. "I have a hand-crank flashlight."

"Urban camping is very popular these days," Maria said.

"I haven't been camping in years," Anna's father added, smiling. "Not since before Anna was born."

"I have so many awesome campout ideas!" Simone told Mr. Hoffman. "We can play Hide-and-Go-Scare, have a ghost hunt, and listen to spooky music. I'll plan everything if you want."

Soon everyone was talking about Simone's ideas. Mr. Hoffman laughed. "It looks like we've chosen our party theme. Thanks, Simone! We'll do it this weekend. I'll send an e-mail to the families that couldn't make it today."

Kaya grabbed Anna's elbow and said, "I can't believe we get to have a sleepover in the garden. It's going to be so scary! I *looooove* ghost stories."

Anna smiled, but her smile felt wobbly and unsure. She thought about how much she loved being in the garden: the bright colors, the warm dirt, the sunshine. Then she thought about the campout: the darkness, the shadows, the strange nighttime noises.

It reminded her of the time she had slept over at her cousins' house back in New York. Their house was haunted. At least, that's what her cousins told her. After that, Anna couldn't fall asleep. All night long she was certain she heard someone moaning behind her, and once she even felt an icy hand touch her cheek, even though her aunt and uncle told her there were no such things as ghosts. When her parents finally arrived to pick her up, Anna's hands wouldn't stop shaking. Her cousins laughed and called her a fraidycat.

A shiver wiggled up Anna's back as she remembered.

"I wonder how you play Hide-and-Go-Scare. Simone has so many spooky ideas!" Kaya clasped her hands together. "Isn't this the best?"

"Sure," Anna said. "The best."

But inside she knew this idea was the W-O-R-S-T! She wished Simone would take her ideas and go to some other garden far, far away.

CHAPTER 2

THE CREEPY CRAWLER CAVE

When Anna shuffled into the kitchen the next morning, she was surprised to find it empty. Her father and Collin were usually making a crazy breakfast, like zucchini granola or eggs banana-dict. Maybe Anna was the first one awake. Lucky her. She knew just what she wanted for breakfast—cereal! Plain, boring cereal topped with freshly picked raspberries from the raspberry bushes in the backyard.

Anna grabbed a big bowl, then slipped on her flip-flops and went outside. When Anna opened the back door, she was surprised to see a faded green tent sitting right next to the raspberry bushes.

Anna took a few steps closer. The cool grass tickled her toes. She wondered who the tent belonged to and how it had gotten into *her* backyard. Anna took a few more steps as a warm summer breeze blew across her face. She wrinkled her nose, because something on the breeze did not smell good. It smelled musty and dusty and damp. G-R-O-S-S!

Was it the tent?

Then Anna heard a swishy sound. Her heart jumped. It reminded Anna of the sound her snow pants made when the legs rubbed together, but it was the middle of the summer, and her snow pants were packed away in a box at the top of her closet. The sound was coming from inside the tent.

Now Anna took a step backward.

Suddenly, a loud unzipping noise ripped through the air, and Collin poked his head out between the tent's two front flaps. "Hi, Anna! Dad found his old tent. Come on in!"

Anna shook her head as her father crawled out of the tent, stood up, and brushed a cob-web from his hair. "There," he said. "Plenty of room for the two of you now." He held the tent flap open. "Go on."

Anna clutched the bowl to her chest. "That's okay," she said, tucking her chin on the rim. "I was going to pick raspberries."

"Bring them in here when you're done!" Collin shouted. "We can eat breakfast in the tent!"

"No way," Anna said. "That thing looks like it's a creepy crawler cave. There are probably spiders in there!"

"Oh," said her father, surprised. "I thought you and Collin would have fun playing in the tent today. Plus, I wanted to give it a chance to air out before we go camping in the garden."

Mr. Fincher waved a hand in front of his nose.

Anna's chest tightened, and for a moment her whole body felt like it was carved out of wood. "I don't want to camp in the garden," she finally said.

Anna's father walked over to her and put his arm around her shoulder. "Aw, Banana, don't be scared. Collin and I will be there with you. Your mom even said she would try to could come too. It'll be just like when we visited Uncle Peter in Philadelphia. We had a great time at the hotel."

Anna shook her head. Camping in the Friendship Garden would be nothing like staying at a hotel. The hotel had bright lights and a game room and an ice machine. And it *didn't* have pitch-black darkness, ghost stories, and no walls. Camping outside would be practically the same thing as sleeping in a haunted house.

Besides, Anna's father didn't know it, but Anna had been scared when she was at the hotel. In the middle of the night, Anna had even asked her houseplants, Chloe, Fern, and Spike, to keep her safe from ghosts, even though she knew they couldn't hear her from so far away.

Anna shook her head. "I'm not going to the party." After she said it, Anna's shoulders sunk. She didn't want to miss the celebration. The Friendship Garden was almost her favorite place in the entire world. But there was no way Anna could sleep outside at night. Especially not after being forced to listen to *ghost* stories.

Anna's father stroked her hair back from her forehead. "Well, I won't make you go if you don't want to."

Anna nodded, but she couldn't tell if her

dad's words made her feel happy or sad. Weren't parents *supposed* to make their kids do things they didn't want to do?

"Do I still get to go?" Collin asked, shining his flashlight all around. "Because I've been making a list of all the bugs I can hunt for at nighttime and it's not fair if I don't get to just because Anna's a fraidycat."

"I'm not a fraidycat! I just like to sleep in my own bed." Anna put one hand on her hip and gave Collin the stink eye. "And besides, you don't need a flashlight in the daytime. It doesn't even do anything."

Collin pointed the flashlight right at Anna, and their father stepped between them. "Whoa," he said. "Settle down. Collin, you still get to go no matter what Anna decides to do. And Anna, maybe you could come to the first part of the campout, and then leave when it's time to go to bed."

Anna tilted her head and thought about it. "Maybe," she said, still thinking. She *would* be happy to sleep at home. But then she'd miss out on everything that happened in the second half of the night. And what would everyone say when they saw Anna going home? They might laugh at her, like her cousins. Simone might call her a baby. No matter which way she imagined it, the whole night came out S-T-I-N-K-Y!

"Now, whether you go or not, you can still have fun playing in the tent with Collin today," her father added. He took the bowl from Anna. "I promise there are no creepy crawlers. Why don't you give it a try while I make you two breakfast to go?"

Anna took a few steps toward the tent and Collin scuttled backward, disappearing from view. As she bent down close to the door flap, the dusty smell made her sneeze.

"Bless you." Collin's voice seemed to come out of nowhere. "I brought an extra flashlight for you."

Anna decided she'd just poke her head inside. She didn't have to go all the way in if she didn't want to. She took a deep breath and peeked through the door flap.

She couldn't believe her eyes!

Inside, the tent was much bigger than it looked from the outside. The floor was covered with colorful blankets and pillows. There was a tiny table in the center of the space piled with art supplies, a bucket in the corner filled with books, and prisms hanging from the ceiling.

Sunlight streamed in from a mesh window at the top of the tent, scattering rainbows all over the walls.

"Dad and I decorated it while you were sleeping." Collin handed her a flashlight.

Anna inched all the way inside and settled herself on a cozy pillow right under the window. The smell wasn't actually so bad anymore. Anna thought she might not even notice it at all if she set up a bouquet of wildflowers on the table. Maybe she'd do that after breakfast.

"Want to see my list?" Collin handed Anna a sheet of paper that said:

fireflies
crickets
katydids
sphinx moth

"It's not done yet. I'm still thinking of

more." Collin held up his copy of *Insects of Illinois*. "I'm going to lead an insect scavenger hunt at the campout."

"You are?" Anna turned on her flashlight and shined it at the prism hanging right in front of her. Rainbows sprang up on the walls of the tent to her left and right. "Who said you get to do that?" Anna couldn't imagine Simone doing an insect scavenger hunt.

"Nobody said." Collin shrugged his shoulders and wrote another bug on his list. "I decided to do it because it will be fun."

Anna chewed her lip. It hadn't occurred to her that other people besides Simone could plan activities for the campout.

Anna looked around the tent and a small smile tugged at the corner of her mouth as her own list began to fill her head.

read bedtime stories to the vegetables

do the nighttime chicken dance

make paper flower lanterns

Anna grabbed a sheet of paper and a marker and began to write everything down. She pictured the Friendship Garden filled with glowing lanterns hanging along the fence. Suddenly, the idea of a campout seemed snuggly instead of scary. Anna even thought of a name for the party: the Comfy, Cozy Campout.

All Anna had to do was make sure everyone did *her* ideas instead of Simone's, and the whole night would be perfect.

CHAPTER 3

GHOST GAMES AND GARDEN GAMES

After lunch the next day, Anna's father and Collin walked Anna over to Kaya's apartment. Well, Mr. Fincher walked, Collin biked, and Anna rode her scooter. Kaya was waiting for Anna by the front door of her building with Daisy, who sat in a soccer chair with a footrest and an umbrella. Kaya stood with one foot on her own scooter.

"Want to ride around the block by ourselves? Daisy said it was okay." Kaya pushed off with the foot that was on the ground and her scooter rolled out onto the sidewalk.

"I said it was okay with me *if* it was okay with Mr. Fincher." Daisy put down her gardening magazine and looked up at Anna's father. "I think if the girls stay together and make a square, they will be fine. They won't be crossing any streets."

"That sounds like a lot of fun, and I'm sure they can handle it. After all, they are almost fourth graders." Anna's father bent down and gave her a kiss on the top of her head. "I'll pick you up at four."

Anna waved at her father as he and Collin headed up the street to the park, but she had barely finished when Kaya sped off ahead of her. Anna tightened the straps of her backpack and raced to keep up. She could hear Daisy calling out behind her, "Stay together!"

Just before she got to the corner, Kaya stopped next to the last maple tree on the block. Anna almost crashed into her. She pulled her scooter alongside Kaya just in the nick of time.

"I had some ideas for the campout," Anna said. Then she asked, "What are you doing?"

Kaya pulled a wrinkly brown paper bag from the pouch she wore strapped around her waist. She opened it and began to scatter peanuts on the ground around the tree.

"Be careful!" Anna said, looking up and down the street. "You might get in trouble for littering."

There were trees all along the street, each one in its own small area marked off by a mini fence. Little green plants grew in the dirt around the tree, and Anna knew that the people in the neighborhood worked hard to keep the street looking nice.

"It's not littering if the peanuts will be gone by morning." Kaya sprinkled a few more for good measure, then folded up the top of the bag and zipped it back in her pouch.

"What do you mean?" Anna asked. "Why will they be gone?"

Kaya pushed off on her scooter and called one word back to Anna. "Crows!"

Anna followed as they rounded the corner

onto the next block. As they approached the third tree, a loud and crazy chorus of cawing began. It sounded like a million birds trying to sing, but they were all off-key. Kaya held out the bag of peanuts to Anna. "Want to help?"

Anna took a handful and tossed them near the base of the tree, while Kaya called to the birds. "Hello, crow!" she screeched, making her voice scratchy and birdlike.

One bird swooped down from the tree, circled around them, and then flew back up to its perch. Anna looked at the branches and saw several other black-feathered shapes staring down at the peanuts.

An older woman wearing a long brown dress wagged a finger at Anna and Kaya as she walked past. "Crows are bad luck!" she said.

Anna shivered even though the sun was shining and the air was hot. Kaya called after the woman, "They are not. Crows are the smartest birds in the world."

Anna looked up at the crows again. One of them tilted its head and looked right at her. She didn't say it, but she had a feeling crows could be smart *and* bad luck. "Let's keep riding," Anna said.

Kaya put the peanuts away, and this time Anna pushed off first.

"I thought of some fun activities for the campout," Anna said. "Do you think we'll *all* be allowed to help plan the party even though it was Simone's idea?"

"Simone thinks she's in charge," Kaya said, swerving her scooter a little bit on purpose, "but the party is for everyone."

Anna breathed a little sigh of relief. She wasn't sure if Kaya would be on her side. The other day at the garden, it had seemed like Kaya really liked Simone's campout ideas.

"It could be really pretty if we made lanterns and hung them up all over the garden." Anna raised her eyebrows and crossed her fingers, which made it a little tricky to keep hold of her handlebars. She really hoped Kaya wanted to make lanterns.

"That's a great idea!" Kaya said. Kaya

and Anna slowed down at the corner before turning onto the last block. Then they sped up again. "I thought of a bunch of things we could do, too," Kaya added. "Like Ghosts in the Graveyard, Spooky Shadow Puppets, and Fear Factor."

Anna's scooter went over a bump and she almost fell. She had to stop for a second, and Kaya got way ahead of her. Anna did not like the sound of Fear Factor. She slowly scooted up to her favorite bookstore, where Kaya was waiting for her to catch up.

"Also," Kaya said, when Anna was finally by her side again, "Daisy has a two-person tent and she said you and I could sleep in it. All by ourselves. *If* your dad says it's okay. I have a book of spooky stories, and we can stay up late reading them to each other!"

Anna looked down at the sidewalk as they scooted their way to the end of the block. Her scooter felt slow and heavy, as if one of the wheels needed oiling. She had wanted to tell Kaya all the rest of her campout ideas, but now they seemed babyish and S-T-U-P-I-D.

"What about the younger kids?" Anna asked. "I bet a lot of your ideas might be too scary for them."

Kaya nodded her head. "I know. I was talking about that with Daisy, and she said we'd probably need to have two sets of activities for the campout: big-kid activities and little-kid activities."

Anna's neck felt hot and itchy with embarrassment. She couldn't go to the campout, even for part of the time, if all of her friends were going to do the big-kid activities and she was going to have to do little-kid activities. *Big* and *little* weren't even the right words, because her brother's friend Jax was a little kid and he'd probably want to do the scariest stuff. And Anna couldn't be the only bigger kid who didn't like to feel spooked. She wished Kaya had called them something different, like Ghost Games and Garden Games. Anna wouldn't feel bad about choosing Garden Games.

"I don't even know if I'm going to go," Anna said as they turned the last corner onto Kaya's block. She could see Daisy up ahead, still reading her magazine and sipping an iced coffee.

"What?" Kaya zoomed her scooter out in front of Anna's, then cut it sideways, blocking Anna's path. "You have to come! Why not?"

Anna thought about telling Kaya the truth: that she didn't like pitch-black darkness and sleeping in places that weren't her bedroom. She especially didn't like ghosts! But she didn't know what Kaya would say. Would she call Anna a fraidycat?

Then Anna remembered that Kaya was her best friend. Kaya would never laugh at her. "I'm afraid of the—"

Anna's confession was interrupted when a bunch of crows began to swoop and caw all around them. Anna screamed and covered her face with her arms. She felt like the birds wanted to peck off her nose, but Kaya giggled. "Don't be scared. That's just their way of saying hello."

Anna slowly lifted her head and watched as the birds flew back down the street. Her heart was pounding. Why did crows have to be so big and loud? Why did she have to be afraid of everything? And why did everyone else feel like being terrified was fun? Anna didn't like that feeling at all.

"I think they recognize me," Kaya told Anna. "I read that some crows are as smart as seven-year-olds."

Anna wondered if that meant they'd want to do the big-kid activities or the little-kid activities.

"Okay, back to the campout. It won't be fun if you're not there." Kaya made a sad face at Anna.

"Bailey and Reed will probably come," she reminded her.

Kaya shook her head. "Not the same."

"I'm scared," Anna finally blurted. "I don't want to do all that creepy stuff, like ghost stories."

Kaya threw her hands in the air. "Why

didn't you just say so? No problem!"

"Really?" This time Anna was so relieved that she felt her eyes getting watery with tears. Of course, Anna had been pretty sure that Kaya would never make fun of her, but it was good to hear the words right from Kaya's mouth.

"All that stuff seems scary because you've never done it before. So all we have to do is get you used to it before the campout." Kaya nodded her head as if it were all settled. "I'll come up with a plan. You'll see. Before you know it, I bet ghost stories will be your favorite thing!"

Kaya raced back to Daisy before Anna could answer. She didn't want to get used to ghost stories. She wanted a Comfy, Cozy Campout.

Anna guessed that everyone was right: She really was a fraidycat.

CHAPTER 4

THE GARDEN GHOST

On Thursday afternoon, Anna met Kaya, Reed, and their friend Bailey at the gates of Shoots and Leaves. Thursdays weren't a regular meeting time for everyone else, but to Anna it always felt like a real Friendship Garden club meeting if all her friends were there.

"Let's check on the Three Sisters Garden,"

Bailey said as Daisy unlocked the gate and let them inside.

"It's not fair that it's called the Three Sisters," Reed said. "Why can't it be the Three Sisters and One Brother?"

Anna laughed. "But corn, beans, and squash have a system. The cornstalks make a pole for the beans to climb up. The beans put the right nutrients in the soil to help the squash, and the squash leaves make shade to stop weeds from taking over the corn. They all grow better when they're together, but there isn't a brother that grows with them. Sorry!"

Anna, Reed, and Bailey headed over to the small square garden bed next to the main Friendship Garden. That was where they had planted their Three Sisters Garden. Kaya always went to the chicken coop first. She liked gardening, but she *loved* animals. Daisy went to work on her own garden.

"Ooh, look!" Anna raced forward to the plants. "Some of the green beans are ripe." Anna plucked one off the vine and took a bite. It was crisp and fresh, and a teeny bit sweet.

"I think green beans are my favorite vegetable," Anna said.

"You say that about every vegetable." Bailey giggled and pulled her own green bean from the vine.

"I guess my real favorite vegetable is whichever one I just picked." Anna shrugged. Vegetables fresh from the garden just tasted better to Anna.

"My favorite vegetable is whichever one I *don't* have to eat," Reed said. "You two can eat my share."

Anna headed over to the little Friendship Garden supply shed to get some small buckets for harvesting. On her way she passed Mr. Hoffman, who was weeding the main Friendship Garden with Simone and Maria.

"Is it okay if we pick some of the green beans?" she asked him.

"Sure," he said. Then, as Anna was walking away, he added, "I found this on the edge of the garden bed last time I was here. I wondered if it belonged to you." Mr. Hoffman held up a rainbow ponytail holder. Anna had never seen it before. She shook her head.

"Nope. Not mine."

"Do you recognize it? Maybe it belongs to one of your friends."

Anna shook her head again. "It doesn't look familiar."

Just then, Kaya came rushing over. "Look what I found!" She opened her fist. A green button, a silver screw, and a marble sat on her palm. "They were sitting on different fence posts around the chicken coop."

"Weird," said Simone. "Who could be leaving all this random stuff around?"

"Maybe we have a garden ghost." Maria stood up, chuckled, and stretched her back.

"A ghost?" Anna repeated.

"I'm just kidding, honey." Maria squeezed Anna's shoulder. "One of the other garden members is probably putting found objects on the garden posts instead of bringing them to the lost and found."

Anna nodded. That made sense.

"O-o-o-r . . ." Simone drew the word out, like she was about to say something really important. She leaned in close so only Anna and Kaya could hear her. "My mom was right. We do have a ghost. He heard about our campout and wants to come, so he's giving us presents in order to get an invitation."

Simone looked all around the garden, cupped one hand around her mouth, and whispered at the sky, "Hey, Garden Ghost! You are hereby invited to our campout!"

Anna knew that Simone was kidding, and she knew that ghosts weren't real—probably—so she didn't know why hearing about ghosts kept making her stomach feel like it was filled with ice water.

Kaya leaned over and whispered in Anna's other ear. "It's just a game," she told her. "A fun, spooky game."

Anna nodded, but she couldn't speak.

"You aren't scared, are you?" Simone suddenly jumped forward and put her fingers in Anna's face. "Boo!" she shouted.

Anna jumped.

Simone cracked up. "Fraidycat! How are you going to make it through the campout if you can't even handle a little joke?"

Anna didn't know what to say. Simone was right. She felt like a B-A-B-Y.

"She's not scared," said Kaya, linking her arm with Anna's. "Everyone jumps if you shout 'boo.'"

"You're not going to wreck the whole campout by being scared of everything, are you?" Simone folded her arms across her chest and stared down at Anna like Anna had just made a mess of things. "My mom said we'd have to stop all my games if anyone got too scared."

Anna swallowed. She didn't know what to say. If she went, she probably *would* wreck the whole campout.

"Anna's going to be fine!" Kaya said, pulling Anna over to the edge of the garden, away from Simone. "Just ignore her. You won't wreck anything." She held out her palm. "Which one do you want?"

Anna looked at the button, the screw,

and the marble. She couldn't decide.

"They're not really from a ghost," Kaya said. "But if they were, it would have to be a nice ghost, right? Mean ghosts don't leave buttons!"

Anna guessed Kaya was right. She picked up the green button and put it in her pocket, but she still wished they were doing a different kind of party. Any other kind of party. Even a homework party or a clean-up-your-bedroom party sounded better than a creepy campout.

When they were back at the Three Sisters Garden, Anna handed out the buckets and started to pick the beans, but Kaya had other ideas.

"We have to come up with a plan," she told Bailey and Reed. "Anna is scared of ghosts and campouts!"

"What?" Reed looked at Anna like he couldn't believe it. "You are?"

Anna's cheeks grew warm, and she bulged her eyes at Kaya. It wasn't a secret, exactly, but why did Kaya have to go and tell the whole world?

"We have to help her get *un*-scared," Kaya added. "Otherwise she isn't going to come!"

"You have to come!" Bailey made a sad face. "My mom already let me buy glow sticks for all of us."

Anna didn't know what to tell her friends. She was too old to be so scared of camping, but she couldn't help herself. Every time she imagined being in the garden at night, in the dark, not being able to tell what was lurking in the shadows, all the hairs on her arms rose up and she shivered.

"I know what we need to do," Reed

announced. "Let's do a practice campout. We can do it during the day, so it won't be as scary, but we'll still do all the other spooky stuff. That way you can see how much fun it is."

Anna wasn't sure she'd ever think scary stuff was fun, but she did like the idea of practicing during the day. "My dad's tent is already set up in my backyard," she confessed.

"Great!" said Bailey. "Let's all ask our parents if we can play at Anna's tomorrow afternoon."

Anna didn't think Reed's idea would work. Having a practice campout in her own backyard in the middle of the afternoon wasn't nearly the same as having a real campout in the garden in the middle of the night, but Anna smiled at her friends. They were just trying to help. "Sounds like fun," she said.

CHAPTER 5

THE COMFY, COZY CAMPOUT

Anna checked and double-checked and triple-checked her father's old tent to make sure all her practice campout supplies were ready. Kaya, Bailey, and Reed might be planning to get Anna used to scary things, but Anna had a plan of her own. She was going to show them that her Comfy, Cozy Campout ideas were so much more fun than their scary ideas. Then they'd change their minds about what they wanted to do at the campout.

Anna straightened the supplies for making lanterns and lined up the flashlights for the game she'd invented: Rainbow Tag. Everyone would shine their flashlights at the prisms, and whenever a person got a rainbow to land on someone's face, they'd get a point. Anna also had a fun recipe for s'mores on a stick. They wouldn't even need a campfire! Y-U-M!

Anna was about to double-check her list of Toast Stories (toast stories were way less scary than ghost stories) when she heard her father's voice calling out to her, "Banana! Your friends are here."

Anna crawled out of the tent and saw Kaya, Reed, and Bailey walking toward her with backpacks and sleeping bags.

"Wow, that's a lot of stuff for a pretend sleepover," Anna said.

"It needs to feel real," Bailey reminded her. "That way you can see that scary sleepover stuff isn't really scary. It's fun!"

"Can I play too?" Collin asked, poking his head out of the back door.

"Actually, I was hoping you would help me," Anna's father said. "I wanted to test out a recipe for pizza on the grill. I thought that might be a good choice for the campout. What do you say?"

"Okay," Collin said, but he didn't seem too happy about it. He followed Mr. Fincher inside as Anna's friends headed into the tent.

"The first thing we have to do is set up," Reed said. "I call the spot under the window." Reed unrolled his sleeping bag and set his backpack behind his pillow. Kaya put her sleeping bag against the back wall, and Bailey arranged her things opposite Reed.

When everything was set up, Reed said, "Okay, we'll start simple." He handed everyone a small sheet of red circle stickers. "This is for the Mosquito Bite game. You have to try to get rid of your stickers by putting them onto other people, but you don't want them to notice you doing it. If they catch you, you have to put that sticker on yourself, plus they get to give you another sticker too. The first person to use up all their stickers wins."

"That actually sounds fun," Anna admitted. Maybe she'd save making lanterns until after the Mosquito Bite game.

"It's not scary at all, right?" Kaya said, patting Anna on the back.

"Right!" Anna agreed, then she thought for a minute. "Hey! Did you just put a sticker on my back?"

"Shoot! I thought that would fool you." Kaya peeled the sticker from Anna's shoulder blade and put it on her own leg. Anna put another sticker right next to it.

"Okay," said Reed. "This game works better when everyone is busy thinking about other things, so let's start gathering firewood."

Kaya and Bailey crawled out of the tent and started to look around Anna's small backyard, but Anna scooted out after them and shook her head. "Um, Reed, we can't have a real fire. And besides, I don't think there's much wood in my backyard."

"I know." Reed picked up a tiny twig as he got out of the tent. He placed it on the edge of Anna's patio. "This part is total pretending, but we can still sit around our twig pile and act like it's a campfire."

Anna nodded and started looking for more twigs. While she was gathering some that were on the ground under the elm tree, she even managed to stick a red dot on the back of Bailey's elbow. When the pretend campfire pile was as big as a football, Kaya called them all to sit in a circle around it.

Kaya put her hand on her knees and leaned forward. "Now, we are going to play a game called Phantom Messenger," she said in a soft and serious voice.

Anna straightened her spine. She wanted to stand up, because she was pretty sure a phantom was the same as a ghost. Maybe she should suggest a game of Rainbow Tag instead. Anna looked around the yard, at the red and yellow flowers stretching toward the sun. She took a deep breath. It was just a game. Anna could handle a ghost game in the middle of the day.

"Here's how it works," Kaya said, keeping her voice low. "I will close my eyes and get a message from the phantom. Then I will whisper it to Reed, who will whisper it to Anna, who will whisper it to Bailey. Then Bailey will say it out loud and we will see if the phantom's message came through."

"That's just like Telephone!" Anna's shoulders relaxed in relief. "I love Telephone."

Bailey patted Anna's knee. "Calling it Phantom Messenger just makes it fun for the campout."

Anna shrugged. She thought the game

was the same amount of fun whatever it was called, but she was glad to learn that games that sounded scary weren't *always* scary for real. They played four rounds, so that each of them could take a turn getting a message from the phantom. Then Bailey said, "Okay, now it's time to play the Wicked Winker." Bailey made her voice sound slow and spooky when she said the name of the game, and Anna felt the skin on her scalp grow tingly.

Maybe now it was time to make the lanterns.

"First, everyone will close their eyes," Bailey explained. "Then I'll tap one person on their shoulder and that person will be the Wicked Winker."

"This game works better with more people," Reed said.

"Shh!" Bailey swatted the air. "Let me finish. Next, we'll all open our eyes, and the Wicked Winker will wink at different people. The winker has to be careful, though, because she doesn't want the others to see her winking. When you get winked at, you have to lie down and play dead, and you are out of the game. If the winker winks everyone out, they win, but if someone catches them, they lose."

This game was a little creepier than Phantom Messenger, but Anna thought it still sounded like it might be fun. She agreed to give it a try. Reed was right, though—they did need more people. As soon as Kaya and Bailey had fallen over to play dead, Anna shouted that Reed was the winker and won the game.

"Do you guys want to try one of my activities now?" Anna asked. She wasn't really worried that any of the games would be too scary for her anymore. She was actually having a lot of fun. But it still couldn't hurt to show her friends that not everything about a campout had to be scary.

"Sure." Kaya nodded. "What do you want to do?"

Anna led them back into the tent and taught them how to play Rainbow Tag. It was much harder than it looked because they could never predict where the rainbows would scatter. They finally stopped playing when Collin poked his head into the tent. His face was covered in rainbows and they all burst out laughing.

"What are you guys playing?" Collin asked. "Can I play?"

"I'll teach you later," Anna told him. "I thought you were helping Dad."

"I was," Collin said. "Now he wants you to do a taste test. It's time for dinner."

"Food!" Reed shouted. He squeezed past Collin and ran out of the tent.

Collin moved out of the way, and Anna, Kaya, and Bailey followed him to the picnic table on the patio. Reed was already several big bites into his first slice. "This is really good, Mr. Fincher. Even if it does have red peppers on it."

Everyone agreed: Grilled pizza was delicious. The crust was nice and crispy, and the cheese was just the right amount of gooey.

Anna was starting to think that maybe she'd been wrong about the campout, and her friends had been right. All she had needed was a practice run to see that the scariness was in her own imagination. She still didn't know if she was going to sleep over, but she could certainly go to the first part and have a lot of F-U-N.

"So," Mr. Fincher said, as everyone was finishing up dinner, "what are you guys going to do next?"

Kaya waggled her eyebrows and gave Bailey and Reed a mischievous grin. "We saved the best for last. Next up? Ghost stories!"

Anna gulped and put her half-finished slice of pizza on her plate. Suddenly she didn't feel hungry anymore.

CHAPTER 6

THE EERIE ECHO

Back in the tent, Kaya climbed into her sleeping bag and sat with it snuggled over her legs. "Get cozy, everyone," she said, passing out the flashlights.

Anna sat on a big comfy pillow and wrapped one blanket around her shoulders and another one around her lap. It didn't stop the shiver from wiggling up her arms when Kaya began the ghost story.

"This story is called 'The Eerie Echo.'" Kaya flicked on her flashlight and held it under her chin so that some parts of her face looked bright and other parts looked shadowy. Anna swallowed. She knew she could tell her friends to stop. They would never make her do something she really didn't want to do, but Anna didn't want to be the fraidycat who had to miss the campout while her friends had all the fun. No, Anna had made it through all the other games and they hadn't been too scary. Maybe ghost stories would turn out to be the same.

"*Once, there were four friends. Maya, Cailey, Hanna, and Reese,*" Kaya began. She looked slowly at each of their faces, as if they were the four friends in the story. "*One day,* they decided to go camping in the woods."

"Ooh!" Bailey said. "The woods."

"They hiked and hiked through the forest, until finally they found a clearing next to a rocky hill. A big ledge jutted out over their heads. They thought that would be good if it rained, so they set up camp. Everything was going great, until they tried to light their campfire. No matter how many matches they used, or how much kindling, they couldn't get it to light. Finally, they gave up and ate cold hot dogs for dinner."

"That's actually not so bad. I've eaten cold hot dogs before." Reed shrugged. "I didn't mean to, but I didn't want to stop playing, so they were cold by the time I got to the table."

Kaya raised an eyebrow at him. It looked spooky in the glow from her flashlight. Reed stopped talking. "Sorry," he whispered.

"Anyway," Kaya continued. *"The cold hot dogs weren't so bad, but when the sun started to set, that's when not having a campfire really became a problem. It was a cloudy night, so there was no moon or stars to brighten the sky. Their camping lantern gave them a little light, but after their third campfire song, the lantern burned out. POOF!"*

Kaya flashed her fingers, and Anna's shoulders flinched a little bit. She snuggled her blanket closer and hoped her friends hadn't noticed.

"The friends had packed more flashlights, but they were inside the tent. Without their camping lantern, the night was so dark they couldn't see where their tent was. It was so dark, they couldn't see one another. It was so dark, they couldn't even see their own hands

if they held them right in front of their faces."

Kaya held her hand right in front of her face, but kept her eyes focused in the distance, as if she was looking right through her fingers. It made Anna's neck tingle.

"'Where are you?' Maya called out.

'Where are you?' a voice called back.

'I'm right next to you,' Hanna whispered, 'you don't need to ask a million times.'

'I only asked once,' Maya said.

Just then there was a loud crack, like a twig snapping. Or something else.

'Reese, was that you?' Cailey shouted.

'Was that you?' another voice called.

'Yes,' Reese said softly. 'It was me. You don't have to ask a million times.'

'I only asked once,' Cailey answered, just as softly. 'Maya, Hanna, did either of you ask?'

'No!' they both said.

'No!' two more people answered."

Anna had been biting her lip, but now she stopped. She had a feeling she knew what the voice was, and it wasn't that scary. Kaya continued the story.

"At first, all four friends froze. Could there be someone out there in the forest with them?

'Who's out there?' Maya called.

'Who's out there?' the voice called back.

'Hello!' Cailey called.

'Hello!' the voice called back.

Hanna laughed, and the sound of giggles and chuckles rang out in the distance as well. All four of the friends had a feeling they knew what was going on.

'You're an echo!' Reese shouted into the night."

Kaya paused. She looked at each of them slowly.

"'*You figured it out!' the voice shouted back.*"

"Aaaah!" Bailey screamed.

"Wait?" Anna asked, shaking her head. "Is that the end?"

Kaya nodded.

"So it wasn't an echo?" Anna asked.

Kaya shrugged.

Anna giggled. She wasn't sure if that was a scary story or not. She was a little scared in the middle, but she didn't feel scared at all by the end. Even when the voice shouted back. That part felt more silly than scary.

"I wonder if we can get an echo in the tent," Reed said. He cupped his hands around his mouth. "Hello!"

"Hello!" a creaky voice answered.

All four friends froze. They looked at one another. Anna's heart was pounding so loudly she wondered if her friends could hear it.

"Echo?" Kaya called out.

"Echo?" the creaky voice answered.

"I think we should go inside the house," Anna whispered. "But I'm scared to leave the tent."

"I think we should try to trap the ghost!" Kaya said, her eyes blazing with excitement.

Reed and Bailey nodded. Anna shook her head.

"Ready?" Reed asked. "On the count of three."

"One!" Bailey shouted. Anna squeezed her hands into fists.

"Two!" Kaya yelled. Anna squeezed her eyes shut.

"Go!" Reed screamed as he tore out of the

tent. Anna planned to stay right where she was, but Bailey and Kaya each took an arm and dragged her out with them. She kept her eyes firmly shut.

"Gotcha!" Reed called out.

Anna heard the sound of crazy laughter. At first her heart lurched, but then she realized the laugh sounded familiar. Anna opened one eye. It was Collin!

"You guys were so scared!" He doubled over with more laughter.

Bailey flopped down on her back in the grass. "That was so fun," she said, her stomach rising and falling because she was still breathing heavily.

Kaya lay down next to her. "Yeah. I love the feeling when you are really scared and then you're not anymore."

Anna's heart was still pounding, but she did feel pretty relieved that the voice was just her brother. Her T-R-I-C-K-Y brother. "You sounded kind of like when Dad plays his trumpet," Anna told Collin. She let out a little giggle. "Badoo, badoo," she said in the same creaky voice. She let out another giggle. Then another, and before she knew it she was laughing like crazy, and soon Kaya, Reed, Bailey, and Collin were too.

Suddenly, four large crows swooped back and forth right above their heads.

"Crows!" Anna shouted. "Run for your lives!"

The four friends ran inside the house, still laughing, with the crows following them the whole way.

Kaya kept shouting, "Hello, crow!"

Anna didn't know if she was terrified or having fun. She didn't know if she liked feeling scared or not. She didn't know if crows were good luck or bad. But she knew one thing: She had the best friends in the world, and if they wanted her to come to the campout, she'd definitely give it a try!

HORRIFYING HOPSCOTCH

On Saturday afternoon when Anna, Collin, and her father arrived for the campout, it was still light outside. The garden looked as green and friendly as it always did. Anna had brought her sleeping bag just in case, but she wasn't going to decide about sleeping over until bedtime. She also brought her three houseplants, Chloe, Fern, and Spike, since she realized that one good thing about sleeping in a garden would be that you could bring your plants with you.

Lastly, she brought supplies for making paper lanterns. Just because she didn't think camping out was as creepy as she used to, that didn't mean she couldn't try to make the campout as comfy and cozy as possible.

When Anna arrived, Kaya was already there. She had set up her two-person tent right next to the chicken coop. Anna wondered if the chickens were excited to have so many people sleeping over.

All along the fence were more tents. Anna's father set their tent up in the back corner next to the Friendship Garden's little shed. They brought the prisms and the pillows and blankets, but not the table. Anna's dad said there

wouldn't be room for the table if they all wound up sleeping over.

"Anna! Collin!" Mr. Hoffman stood by a portable barbecue wearing an apron and a chef's hat. "I'm so glad you're here! Are you going to help me and your father grill the pizza?"

"I am!" Collin shouted. "I discovered I actually like eggplant. But only if it's on pizza."

Anna shook her head. "I'm going to see if anyone wants to make lanterns with me."

Mr. Hoffman gave her a thumbs-up and Anna went to find her friends. They set the box of lantern-making supplies on the ledge of the Friendship Garden and started unpacking. Anna had brought enough paper bags for everyone at the campout, just in case, but she didn't want to make a big announcement about it. She could just imagine Simone telling everyone what a stupid idea lanterns were and then convincing them to play Horrifying Horror Hopscotch or Terrifying Terror Tag. She'd probably tell everyone that Anna was ruining the campout.

Anna was setting out glue sticks when Simone came over, holding her hands behind her back. "Guess what I've got?" she said.

"S'mores?" Reed asked hopefully.

"What?" Simone rolled her eyes. "We won't have s'mores until after it's dark out. No. Guess again."

"A flashlight?" Bailey guessed.

Simone shook her head. "Nope."

"A kitten?" Kaya clasped her hands together. "Please let it be a kitten."

Simone laughed. "You guys aren't even close."

"It's obviously something scary," Anna

muttered to herself. She quietly tucked some of the art supplies back into the box, hoping Simone wouldn't notice them.

Simone held her hands out in front and opened her palms. "The garden ghost brought us more presents!"

Anna saw a scrap of silver ribbon, a bolt, a piece of purple glass, part of a zipper, and a bent paper clip.

"They were all over the garden when I got here today. Sitting on different garden ledges. I think the ghost really wants to meet us."

Anna's skin felt cold, even though the sun was shining and it was still warm out. "There're no such things as ghosts," she muttered.

"Well, *someone* is leaving these presents." Simone held her hands right in front of Anna's face. "And they don't seem like the kind of things that a *person* would leave. Are you scared?"

Anna looked down at her knees. She was almost 100 percent sure there were no such things as ghosts, and besides, even if Simone was right, what she was saying didn't make any sense. If a ghost used to be a person, then they *would* leave person gifts. Anna slowly slid the bags back into the box as Kaya said, "I've been finding funny things on my front stoop, too. Yesterday I found the spring from a pen. Maybe the ghost is following me!"

But Simone didn't answer Kaya. She was looking at Anna. "What's all that stuff?" she asked, pointing to the box.

Anna froze. She wanted to hide the box behind her back, but she knew it was too late for that. Still, she didn't want to tell Simone about lantern making. Simone would tease her. She would ruin the lantern project. Anna was sure of it.

"It's nothing," Anna said. "Just a few things I brought for the campout."

"Anna's teaching us how to make paper lanterns!" Kaya explained, and Anna felt her stomach drop down to her knees. Kaya hadn't known Anna wanted the lanterns to be a secret from Simone, but Anna still felt like poking her in the ribs. Lately it felt like Kaya was blabbing everything about Anna.

"Yeah. Anna wants us to hang lanterns all over the garden fence," Bailey added.

Simone looked at the box, then she looked at the fence. Anna felt her shoulders tense. Any second now Simone would say something like, *I haven't made a lantern since I was in preschool.* But instead Simone said, "Lanterns? Do you have enough supplies for me to make one too?"

Anna blinked. "You want to make a lantern?"

"Yeah! It'll be so cool in the dark with lanterns all over the place. They'll look like ghost lights."

Anna almost laughed out loud. Of course Simone would imagine them as something scary! But Anna realized it didn't matter how Simone imagined the lanterns. Anna could still see them as cozy and comfy. "Sure!" Anna opened the box and handed Simone a paper bag, scissors, tissue paper, and glue.

She showed Simone how to fold the bag to cut shapes out of it, then how to glue the tissue over the holes. Then, when Simone folded the

bag with her finger in the way, Anna added, "Watch your fingers, you don't want to cut yourself." Anna smiled. That was exactly what Simone had said to her the other day when they were picking cabbage. She guessed Simone wasn't so old after all. Or maybe Anna wasn't such a baby.

Pretty soon a lot of other kids came over and wanted to make lanterns. Anna passed out the supplies, gave the instructions, and when kids started to finish, Anna added battery-operated tea lights and hung them on the fence with pipe cleaners. The sun was sinking lower in the sky, and the lanterns looked cheerful and warm, like they were smiling on the garden.

Anna was smiling back at the lanterns when she heard Maria shout, "Oh no!"

Anna whirled around and saw Maria over by the Three Sisters Garden inspecting the corn. Anna, Kaya, Bailey, and Reed raced over. And, on the other side of the garden, Mr. Hoffman handed Anna's father the spatula and hurried to Maria's side.

"What is it?" he asked.

"Your corn!" Maria made a sad face. "We must have some kind of critter again because most of your ears have been split open and eaten."

"Squirrels?" Mr. Hoffman asked.

Maria shrugged. "Maybe, but I've been spraying around the garden with hot pepper spray, and I haven't noticed any squirrels around here for a long time."

"Does this mean there won't be any corn on the cob this fall?" Reed asked.

"There are some stalks that aren't damaged." Anna pointed to the corn on the other side of the Three Sisters bed. "Maybe if we figure out who the thief is, we can stop it before it eats the rest of the corn."

"And before it eats the rest of the gardens!" Maria said. "Critters usually tell their friends. This could grow into a huge problem."

Maria shook her head and she and Mr.

Hoffman walked over to Maria's office shed, trying to figure out what to do.

Anna turned around and realized Simone was standing right behind her.

"Maybe it was the *ghost*," Simone said, leaning over Anna and making her voice spooky.

"Eating corn?" Anna asked. She put her hands on her hips. A corn-eating ghost sounded more silly than scary.

"I don't think ghosts can eat corn," Bailey agreed.

Simone tilted her head and thought about it. "Probably not, but I bet the ghost knows who ate the corn. We should try to talk to it. You know, communicate with the spirit world. That would totally be a fun thing to do at a campout. We'll have to wait until it's really dark, though."

Anna did not like the sound of that at all. She was definitely going home before Simone tried to talk to a ghost. She just hoped her mother arrived in time.

"Cool," Kaya said to Simone. "I'm in!"

"Me too," said Reed.

"Let's talk to the friendly ghost!" Bailey pumped her fist in the air. "What about you, Anna?"

Anna opened her mouth, but nothing came out. She wasn't going to do it, but she didn't want to tell everyone. Not when Simone would say that Anna was wrecking the camp-out. Besides, her friends thought she wasn't a fraidycat anymore. She didn't want to disappoint them.

Suddenly, a jangly *ding-a-ling* sound filled

the air. Anna's father was ringing a triangle and calling, "Come and get it!"

"Pizza!" Anna cried. Her friends jumped up and raced over to the grill, their question totally forgotten. Hopefully by the time they remembered, Anna would be tucked safely in her own bed. At home.

CHAPTER 8

THE GARDEN GHOST AGAIN

After dinner, Collin found a couple of kids who wanted to try his insect scavenger hunt. The fireflies were starting to light up the garden and Anna thought she'd never seen anything so pretty. Maybe being in the garden in the pitch-black dark sounded scary, but being in the garden in the almost-dark was kind of nice.

The grown-ups pulled out the big metal fire pit and were discussing the best way to start a fire. Anna had no idea what the teepee method or the log cabin method meant, but everyone seemed to have a different idea. It might be a while before she could make her s'more.

Anna wanted to read bedtime stories to the garden while she was waiting. She bet if she suggested they also read to the chickens, Kaya would want to do it too. She was just about to look for her book of silly bedtime stories when Simone grabbed her arm.

"*Psst*," Simone whispered. "It's time."

Anna's heart *ka-thunk*ed. She looked at the gate of Shoots and Leaves, hoping her mother would arrive in the nick of time, but no one was there except the shadows of the two trees guarding the entrance.

"I was about to do something else," Anna said, taking a step toward her tent.

Simone didn't let go. "Everyone's waiting for you." She pointed to the dark front corner of the garden, right underneath the branches of the big maple tree. Kaya, Reed, Bailey, and Imani were sitting in a circle. Kaya waved her arm to beckon Anna over. Anna gulped.

"Are you coming?" Simone asked. "Or should I tell everyone to forget the whole thing?"

Anna wanted to say no, to go in her tent and zip up the flap and stay there until her mother arrived to save her. But she didn't want Simone to call her a baby, and she didn't want her friends to think she was still a fraidycat.

Anna looked over her shoulder at her father piling logs in the fire pit. He was only a couple of garden beds away from her. If anything got too scary, Anna could call his name and he'd be right over. Besides, ghosts weren't real. Anna was 99 percent sure.

Anna sighed. She let Simone lead her to the circle of kids sitting at the front of the garden.

"Okay," Simone said after she and Anna settled themselves cross-legged in the empty space between Imani and Kaya. "We are going to communicate with the Garden Ghost."

Simone got up, removed her lantern from the garden fence, and set it down in the center of the circle. Then she emptied her pockets of all the trinkets the ghost had left over the past week and scattered them around the lantern. "Kaya?" she said.

Kaya emptied her pockets and put the purple star charm, the marble, the screw, and the spring next to the other items.

Anna *did* think it was weird that all those things had been found around the garden this week when they had never found little things like that before, but that didn't mean there was a ghost. She hoped.

"Good." Simone nodded. "Now we hold hands."

Simone took Anna's left hand and Kaya took her right. Anna realized that her palms were all sweaty. She quickly broke the circle for a second to wipe them on her shirt.

"Ghost of the garden," Simone called out in a low voice, "we thank you for your gifts!"

Simone squeezed Anna's hand. Then she leaned over and said, "Now you say 'thank you' and squeeze Kaya's hand until we go all around the circle."

"Um, thank you," Anna said, even though

she felt totally ridiculous talking to a not-real ghost. "I really like the green button." She squeezed Kaya's hand.

When everyone had taken a turn, Simone said, "We hope that you will gift us with your presence."

"The ghost already gave us presents!" Reed shook his head. "You're being kind of greedy. The ghost probably won't talk to us if we're greedy."

"Not presents!" Simone did her famous eye roll. "*Presence.* That means 'being here.' We want the ghost to visit us." Simone huffed out a breath. "Never mind."

She switched back to her low ghost-talking voice. "We hope that you will come say hello."

This time Simone squeezed Imani's hand, who said, "Please talk to us." The hand squeeze went around the circle in the opposite direction until it was Anna's turn. Anna said, "You don't have to visit us if you don't want to."

Simone lifted both hands halfway up in the air, taking Anna's and Imani's hands with her. "Now, we'll all raise our hands, close our eyes, and whisper 'welcome' over and over until we get a sign."

Anna watched as everyone closed their eyes. She listened as everyone whispered, "Welcome, welcome, welcome." She wondered how Simone knew that this was the way you were supposed to talk with a ghost, and she realized Simone was probably just making the whole thing up. Anyway, everyone had their eyes closed, and everyone was whispering, but nothing was happening. No ghost was talking to them.

It didn't seem like much fun, but it also didn't seem too scary anymore, so Anna closed her eyes and began to whisper with her friends. "Welcome, welcome, welcome."

A breeze wafted across the circle and lifted the hair off the back of Anna's neck. A couple of people stopped whispering for a second, but Simone said, "Keep going."

They kept whispering "Welcome, welcome, welcome" and the breeze grew stronger. Anna heard a sound that she thought might be Simone's lantern falling over. She opened one eye. Yep, she'd been right. She closed her eye and whispered some more. Suddenly, the breeze stopped.

"Aaallooo-rooo," a voice creaked in the night.

Now everyone stopped whispering and opened their eyes.

"Who did that?" Simone said. "Not funny!"

"Allo-ro," the voice creaked again. This time, with all their eyes open, they knew it hadn't been anyone in the circle playing a trick.

Simone dropped Anna's hand and scooted back from the circle a bit. "Who's doing that?" Her eyes darted around the garden, trying to find the speaker.

"I bet it's Collin!" Bailey said. "He tricked us like that once before."

Everyone scanned the garden, looking for Anna's brother.

"There he is," Reed said, pointing all the way across to the other corner. Collin was looking at a firefly in a jar with Jax.

"Allo, allo," the voice creaked loudly. It definitely wasn't Collin.

Everyone looked at one another. Anna

thought they must be wondering the same thing. If it wasn't Collin, who was making that noise?

"Aww! Allo-ro."

"It's a ghost!" Simone screamed. "Help!" She jumped up and ran over to her mother at the fire pit. Imani said, "I want to go home." She scrambled after Simone.

Anna's skin burst out in goose bumps, but her body felt very still. Her ears were pricked. What was going on?

Bailey wiped a tear from her eye and Kaya bit her lip. Reed shouted, "Go away, ghost." Then he covered his head with his hands.

Anna's heart beat hard in her chest. A breeze brushed the hairs poking out on her arms. Was a ghost really saying hello? She thought about the Eerie Echo story. The echo that wasn't an echo. Could this be a ghost that wasn't a ghost?

"Hello?" Anna called out. Her voice sounded shaky.

Reed said, "Shhh!"

"Allo!" the voice answered. It sounded like it was coming from above.

Anna leaned back. Her heart beat even faster. "Hello!"

"Aww. Allo." The voice was definitely coming from above. Suddenly, Anna noticed a dark shadow with two red eyes. She was about to scream when the shadow moved. Like a big clap of thunder, the answer hit Anna. She figured it out!

"Kaya!" Anna said, hugging her friend and laughing. "You were right! Crows really are the smartest birds in the world! I think that one figured out how to say hello!" Anna pointed at the bird in the tree above her.

"Allo!" it called out to them. "Allo-ro."

"It's saying 'Hello, crow!' Just like I say!" Kaya clapped her hands. "Omigosh! I bet that's who's been leaving all the presents! I read that crows do that sometimes for people who feed them."

"I bet that's who ate our corn, too," Anna said, frowning.

"No problem," said Reed. "We'll put a scarecrow in the Three Sisters Garden. Then it really will be the Three Sisters and One Brother."

Anna laughed as Maria came over, pulling Simone by the hand. Simone had her other hand wrapped around her mother's arm.

"So what's this I hear about a ghost in the

garden? Are you guys okay?" Maria asked.

"We're fine," Anna said. "I figured out that our garden ghost is really a crow." Anna pointed up in the tree. "Kaya's been feeding the crows down the block, and this one just wanted to say thank you."

Simone looked up in the tree and shuddered. "A crow?" She held her mom's arm even tighter. "Crows freak me out!"

Maria laughed. "Good for you, Anna, for keeping your head." Maria tugged Simone back in the other direction. "Come on, you scaredy-cat, let's go roast a marshmallow."

Reed's eyes grew wide. "Is it time for s'mores?"

Maria nodded, and Reed took off running.

They all followed him to the fire pit. Most people were sitting around in camp chairs or on the edges of garden beds since only four or five could roast a marshmallow at one time. Daisy brought her guitar and was leading everyone in singing "On Top of Spaghetti." Anna started singing along when she felt a hand on her shoulder. For a second, she jumped, but when Anna turned around, she saw her mother.

"Mom!" She gave her mother a big hug. "You're here."

"What did I miss?" Anna's mom gave her a kiss on her forehead. "Do I have time to eat a s'more or do you want to go home right away?"

Anna looked around the garden. The sky was pitch-black, but the moon was bright. The lanterns glowed along the fence, and the fire in the fire pit gave a happy orange glow to all the friendly faces gathered around it. There were still shadows and no walls, but Anna realized the shadows felt calm and quiet, not spooky. The lack of walls actually made Anna feel big and open, like when she was staring at stars in the sky. Even if they hadn't done all of Anna's activities, it really was a Comfy, Cozy Campout.

"Actually," Anna told her mother. "I think I want to stay."

"You do?" her mother asked. "Well, that's great."

"Yep," Anna agreed. Campouts were G-R-E-A-T!

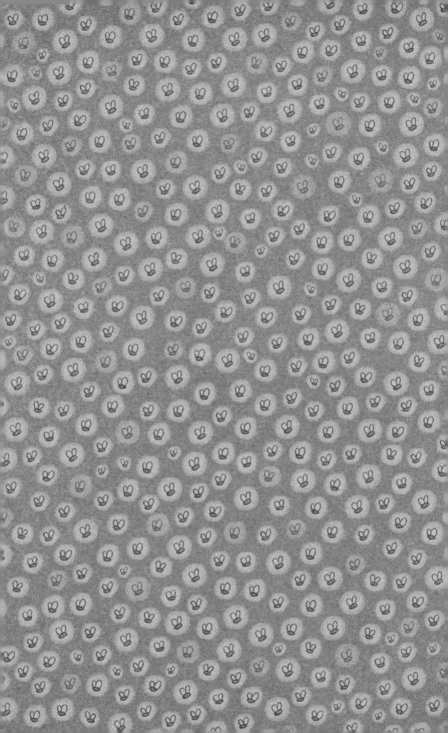

ACTIVITY: **PAPER BAG LANTERN**

What you will need:

Lunch-size paper bag (any color will work, but white lets the most light through)

Multicolored tissue squares (approximately 1-inch square; you can cut these yourself from tissue paper or buy them already cut)

Scissors

Glue stick

LED tea lights

What you will do:

OPTION ONE

Fold the paper bag in half and use the scissors to cut out two or three interesting shapes down the centerfold. When you open the bag, it will have matching holes on the front and back.

Use the glue stick to attach tissue paper over the holes. You can attach the tissue to the outside of the bag, or if you don't want the edges to show, attach it to the inside of the bag.

Next, when the glue is dry, turn on your tea light and put it at the bottom of your bag. Set your lantern outside or in a dark room at night. Enjoy the beautiful glow.

OPTION TWO

The colors from the tissue paper will glow brightest if you cut holes in the bag, but they will still glow even if you do not. If you don't want to bother with cutting holes, just glue the tissue squares right onto the bag in any design you'd like. When the glue is dry, follow the rest of step three above and see how cozy and comfy your lantern makes you feel.

RECIPE: **HOMEMADE PIZZA SAUCE**

Ingredients:

10 small tomatoes

1 cup water

2 tablespoons olive oil

1/4 cup white sugar

2 tablespoons garlic salt

1 tablespoon white vinegar

1 large pot

a food processor or blender

Instructions:

1. Place the tomatoes, water, and olive oil in a blender or food processor. Make sure the lid is on tightly, then blend until the mixture is smooth.

2. Move the tomato mixture to a large pot.

Pour it slowly so it doesn't splash tomatoes all over the place!

3. With an adult helping you, stir the sugar, garlic salt, and vinegar into the tomato mixture and bring to a boil. Reduce the heat to medium-low and simmer until thickened, one to two hours, stirring occasionally.

4. Let the tomato sauce cool for another hour.

OPTIONAL:

After the sauce has cooled, pour your tomato sauce back into a clean blender or food processor no more than half full. Make sure the lid is on and puree your sauce again until it is perfectly smooth. You might need to do this in batches so the blender doesn't get overfull.

Extra sauce can be frozen in freezer bags.

Once your sauce is done, you are ready to make a pizza! You can use store-bought crust, English muffins, bagels, or make a crust from scratch. Add your special sauce, a sprinkling of mozzarella, and your favorite toppings. Y-U-M!

Did you LOVE reading this book?

Visit the Whyville...

IN THE MIDDLE BOOK HIVE

Where you can:

◯ Discover great books!

◯ Meet new friends!

◯ Read exclusive sneak peeks and more!

Log on to visit now!
bookhive.whyville.net

Looking for another great book?
Find it
IN THE MIDDLE.

Fun, fantastic books for kids
in the in-be**TWEEN** age.

IntheMiddleBooks.com

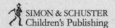